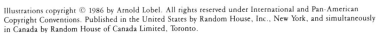

Library of Congress Cataloging-in-Publication Data:
Mother Goose. Selections. The just right Mother Goose. (A Just right book) SUMMARY: An illustrated collection of fifty nursery rhymes, including ("Peter Piper," "She Sells Sea Shells," "Hector Protector," and "Three Blind Mice." 1. Nursery rhymes. 2. Children's poetry. [1. Nursery rhymes] I. Lobel, Arnold, ill. II. Title. III. Series: Just right book (New York, N.Y.) PZ8.3.M85 1989 398'.8 88-43156 ISBN: 0-394-82860-7 (trade); 0-394-92860-1 (lib. bdg.)

Manufactured in the United States of America 1 2 3 4 5 6 7 8 9 0

JUST RIGHT BOOKS is a trademark of Random House, Inc.

A Just Right Book

THE JUST RIGHT
MOTHER GOOSE

Illustrated by
ARNOLD LOBEL

Random House 🏠 New York

Little Bo-Peep has lost her sheep
And doesn't know where to find them;
Leave them alone,
And they'll come home
Bringing their tails behind them.

Little Bo-Peep fell fast asleep
And dreamed she heard them bleating;
But when she awoke,
She found it a joke,
For they were still a-fleeting.

Then up she took her little crook,
Determined for to find them;
She found them indeed,
But it made her heart bleed,
For they'd left their tails behind them.

It happened one day,
As Bo-Peep did stray
Into a meadow hard by;
There she espied their tails side by side,
All hung on a tree to dry.

She heaved a sigh, and wiped her eye,
And over the hillocks went rambling,
And tried what she could,
As a shepherdess should,
To tack again each to its lambkin.

All work and no play makes Jack a dull boy;
All play and no work makes Jack a mere toy.

A diller, a dollar,
A ten o'clock scholar,
What makes you come so soon?
You used to come at ten o'clock,
And now you come at noon.

Mary had a little lamb,
Its fleece was white as snow;
And everywhere that Mary went
The lamb was sure to go.

It followed her to school one day,
That was against the rule;
It made the children laugh and play
To see a lamb in school.

Why does the lamb love Mary so?
The eager children cry;
Why, Mary loves the lamb, you know,
The teacher did reply.

Yankee Doodle went to town,
Riding on a pony.
Stuck a feather in his hat
And called it macaroni.

Yankee Doodle keep it up,
Yankee Doodle dandy.
Mind the music and the step
And with the girls be handy.

Moses supposes his toeses are roses,
But Moses supposes erroneously;
For nobody's toeses are posies of roses
As Moses supposes his toeses to be.

Lucy Locket lost her pocket,
Kitty Fisher found it;
Not a penny was there in it,
Only ribbon round it.

Diddlety, diddlety, dumpty,
The cat ran up the plum tree;
Half a crown
To fetch her down,
Diddlety, diddlety, dumpty.

There was a little green house,
And in the little green house
There was a little brown house,
And in the little brown house
There was a little yellow house,
And in the little yellow house
There was a little white house,
And in the little white house
There was a little heart.

Little Tommy Tucker
Sings for his supper:
What shall we give him?
White bread and butter.

How shall he cut it
Without even a knife?
How will he be married
Without even a wife?

Handy-spandy,
Jack-a-Dandy,
Loves plum cake
And sugar candy.
He bought some
At a grocer's shop,
And out he came,
Hop, hop, hop, hop.

Jack Sprat could eat no fat,
His wife could eat no lean,
And so between them both, you see,
They licked the platter clean.

Mary had a pretty bird,
Feathers bright and yellow,
Slender legs, upon my word,
He was a pretty fellow.

The sweetest notes he always sang,
Which much delighted Mary;
And near the cage she'd ever sit
To hear her own canary.

I'll sing you a song,
Though not very long,
Yet I think it as pretty as any;
Put your hand in your purse,
You'll never be worse,
And give the poor singer a penny.

She sells sea shells on the seashore;
The shells that she sells are sea shells I'm sure.
So if she sells sea shells on the seashore,
I'm sure that the shells are seashore shells.

How much wood would a woodchuck chuck
If a woodchuck could chuck wood?
He would chuck as much wood
As a woodchuck could chuck
If a woodchuck could chuck wood.

Peter Piper picked a peck of pickled peppers;
A peck of pickled peppers Peter Piper picked;
If Peter Piper picked a peck of pickled peppers,
Where's the peck of pickled peppers
Peter Piper picked?

Doctor Foster went to Gloucester in a shower of rain;
He stepped in a puddle, right up to his middle,
And never went there again.

I do not like thee, Doctor Fell,
The reason why I cannot tell;
But this I know, and know full well,
I do not like thee, Doctor Fell.

An apple a day
Sends the doctor away.

How many days has my baby to play?
Saturday, Sunday, Monday,
Tuesday, Wednesday, Thursday, Friday,
Saturday, Sunday, Monday.

Georgie Porgie, pudding and pie,
Kissed the girls and made them cry;
When the boys came out to play,
Georgie Porgie ran away.

Hector Protector was dressed all in green;
Hector Protector was sent to the queen.
The queen did not like him,
No more did the king;
So Hector Protector was sent back again.

Little drops of water, little grains of sand,
Make the mighty ocean and the pleasant land.

ree blind mice,
ree blind mice,
e how they run!
e how they run!
ey all ran after the farmer's wife,
ho cut off their tails with a carving knife;
d you ever see such a sight in your life
three blind mice?

Terence McDiddler,
The three-stringed fiddler,
Can charm, if you please,
The fish from the seas.

Mollie, my sister, and I fell out,
And what do you think it was all about?
She loved coffee, and I loved tea,
And that was the reason we couldn't agree.

Jack be nimble,
Jack be quick,
Jack jump over
The candlestick.

Here am I,
Little Jumping Joan;
When nobody's with me
I'm all alone.

If you wish to live and thrive,
Let the spider walk alive.

Fishy, fishy in the brook,
Daddy catch him on a hook,
Mommy fry him in a pan,
Johnny eat him like a man.

Milkman, milkman, where have you been?
In buttermilk channel up to my chin.
I spilled my milk and I spoiled my clothes
And got a long icicle hung to my nose.

Whistle, daughter, whistle,
And you shall have a sheep.
I cannot whistle, Mother,
Neither can I sleep.

Whistle, daughter, whistle,
And you shall have a cow.
I cannot whistle, Mother,
Neither know I how.

Whistle, daughter, whistle,
And you shall have a man.
I cannot whistle, Mother,
But I'll do the best I can.

A whistling girl and a flock of sheep
Are two good things for a farmer to keep.

On Saturday night shall be my care
To powder my locks and curl my hair;
On Sunday morning my love will come in,
When he will marry me with a gold ring.

Curly locks, Curly locks,
Wilt thou be mine?
Thou shalt not wash dishes
Nor yet feed the swine,
But sit on a cushion
And sew a fine seam,
And feed upon strawberries,
Sugar, and cream.

Pat a cake, pat a cake, baker's man,
Bake me a cake as fast as you can.
Pat it and prick it, and mark it with B,
And put it in the oven for Baby and me.

Ring-a-ring-a-roses,
A pocket full of posies;
Hush! Hush! Hush! Hush!
We've all tumbled down.

Cobbler, cobbler, mend my shoe,
Yes, good master, that I'll do.
Stitch it up and stitch it down,
And then I'll give you half a crown.

Cobbler, cobbler, mend my shoe,
Get it done by half-past two;
Half-past two, it can't be done,
Get it done by half-past one.

Birds of a feather will flock together,
And so will pigs and swine;

Rats and mice will have their choice,
And so will I have mine.

I married a wife by the light of the moon,
A tidy housewife, a tidy one;
She never gets up until it is noon,
And I hope she'll prove a tidy one.

Elsie Marley has grown so fine,
She won't get up to serve the swine,
But lies in bed till eight or nine,
And surely she does take her time.

There was a crooked man,
And he walked a crooked mile.
He found a crooked sixpence
Against a crooked stile;
He bought a crooked cat,
Which caught a crooked mouse,
And they all lived together
In a little crooked house.

I like little pussy,
Her coat is so warm,
And if I don't hurt her,
She'll do me no harm.
So I'll not pull her tail,
Nor drive her away,

But pussy and I
Very gently will play.
She shall sit by my side,
And I'll give her some food
And pussy will love me
Because I am good.

Little Tee Wee,　　And while afloat
He went to sea　　The little boat bended
In an open boat.　　And my story's ended.

Pussycat, pussycat, where have you been?
I've been to London to visit the queen.
Pussycat, pussycat, what did you do there?
I frightened a little mouse under her chair.

Little Tommy Tittlemouse
Lived in a little house;
He caught fishes
In other men's ditches.

The cock crows in the morn
To tell us to rise,
And he that lies late
Will never be wise:

For early to bed
And early to rise
Is the way to be healthy
And wealthy and wise.

One for the money, and two for the show, three to make ready, and four to go.

Sleep, baby, sleep,
Thy father guards the sheep;
Thy mother shakes the dreamland tree
And from it fall sweet dreams for thee,
Sleep, baby, sleep.

Sleep, baby, sleep,
Our cottage vale is deep;
The little lamb is on the green,
With woolly fleece so soft and clean—
Sleep, baby, sleep.

Sleep, baby, sleep,
Down where the woodbines creep;
Be always like the lamb so mild,
A kind and sweet and gentle child,
Sleep, baby, sleep.